MIRIAM COHEN

DON'T EAT
TOO MUCH
TURKEY!

ILLUSTRATED BY
LILLIAN HOBAN

A Young Yearling Book

Published by
Dell Publishing
a division of
Bantam Doubleday Dell Publishing Group, Inc.
1540 Broadway
New York, New York 10036

ISBN: 0-440-40106-2

Reprinted by arrangement with Greenwillow Books, a division of William Morrow & Company, Inc.

Printed in the United States of America

November 1988

13   12   11   10   9   8   7   6   5

WES

For Angelia Di Scala,
my wonderful Sunnyside librarian,
who asked me to write this book

It was the end of November. Their teacher read
a story to First Grade about the Pilgrims and
the first Thanksgiving. Then everybody made
Thanksgiving pictures.

When Louie was walking home, some big boys grabbed his turkey picture. They tore it and threw it down.

Jim and Paul and George saw them do it.
They tried to fix Louie's picture,
then they walked him home.

The next day, Jim and Paul started to tell what had happened to Louie, but Anna Maria interrupted. "I'm writing a play about Thanksgiving.

"You're the Indians," she told Margaret and
   Sara, Willy and Sammy, George and Jim.
"I'm the leader of the Pilgrims, and Paul
   and Louie are Pilgrims, too."

"First, I say, 'The Pilgrims have decided to invite
you to a party.'" She pushed the Indians into
their chairs.
"Here is the turkey and mashed potatoes,
and here is a delicious pumpkin pie I made."

"No, thanks," Sammy said. "My mother always makes coconut cream pie at Thanksgiving." "That's wrong! It's got to be pumpkin," said Anna Maria.

"Hey," Willy said, "where's
the sweet potatoes with
marshmallows?"
"Here is the cranberry sauce,"
said Anna Maria.

"I want the kind with no skins!" Jim said.
"And *no* broccoli!" George cried.
"The Indians aren't supposed to talk!"
shouted Anna Maria.

Danny didn't have a part in the play. So he said,
"I'll be Christopher Columbus and find America."
And Sara said, "I'm not an Indian anymore.
I'm the Statue of Liberty!"

"No! No! No!" Anna Maria cried. Then Willy started showing Sammy how to dance "The Robot." Everybody told Anna Maria, "We don't want to be in this dumb play anyhow."

The teacher brought out
a big brown cardboard box.

"How about making a giant
class turkey?" she said.

In her scrap bag the kids found some long
red socks for the legs, and red felt for under
the turkey's chin.
A brown paper bag was the head, and a funnel
was the beak.

Anna Maria stopped writing her play.
"I'm first to be the turkey!" she said.

But Danny shouted, "Don't let her!
That big bossy stupid!
In nursery school she was bothering me,
in kindergarten she was bothering me!
All my life she's been bothering me!"

"Now, now," the teacher said.
"She *did* ask first.
  Why don't we take turns?"

"We don't want turns with her.
She can have it." Everybody
walked away. The teacher helped
Anna Maria put on the turkey.

Anna Maria went around saying,
"Gobble, gobble, gobble."
But no one would listen.
No one would look at her.

Then Jim whispered in the turkey's funnel,
"Let Louie be the turkey now."
"Why should I? I asked first," Anna Maria said.

But she went over to Louie and said,
"Here, you want to be the turkey? It's very
boring, but you'd probably like it."
"Oh, yes!" said Louie.

Then the kids moved over so that Anna Maria could help make turkey cookies. Willy and Sammy painted a big mural of the Pilgrims and the Indians.

It showed them eating turkey, cranberry sauce, sweet potatoes with marshmallows, pumpkin pie, *and* coconut cream pie. It showed them having a baseball game afterwards. One team was "The Pilgrims" and one was "The Indians."

When the cookies were baked
they all ate turkey cookies
and drank cranberry juice
until it was time to go home
for Thanksgiving vacation.

Louie's grandfather looked
in the door. He had come
to take Louie to his music
lesson.

"Don't tell your grandfather it's you,"
whispered Paul.
And everyone shouted, "Louie isn't here!"
Louie's grandfather looked worried.

Then Louie jumped up and hugged him.
"Grandfather, it's me!" he said.
Everyone laughed.

Soon it was time for everybody to go home.
"Happy Thanksgiving!" they all shouted.
"Don't eat too much turkey!
"Happy Thanksgiving!"